LOTTA MAKES A MESS!

ASTRID LINDGREN

LOTTA MAKES A MESS!

Translated by Tom Geddes
Illustrated by Tony Ross

OXFORD
UNIVERSITY PRESS

OXFORD
UNIVERSITY PRESS

Great Clarendon Street, Oxford OX2 6DP
Oxford University Press is a department of the University of Oxford.
It furthers the University's objective of excellence in research, scholarship,
and education by publishing worldwide in
Oxford New York
Auckland Cape Town Dar es Salaam Hong Kong Karachi
Kuala Lumpur Madrid Melbourne Mexico City Nairobi
New Delhi Shanghai Taipei Toronto
With offices in
Argentina Austria Brazil Chile Czech Republic France Greece
Guatemala Hungary Italy Japan Poland Portugal Singapore
South Korea Switzerland Thailand Turkey Ukraine Vietnam
Oxford is a registered trade mark of Oxford University Press
in the UK and in certain other countries

Text © Astrid Lindgren 1962, 2001 Saltkråkan AB
Illustrations © Tony Ross 2008

Translated from the Swedish by Tom Geddes
English translation © Tom Geddes 2008

This translation of *Lotta Makes a Mess* originally published in Swedish,
published by arrangement with Saltkråkan Förvaltning AB

The moral rights of the author, illustrator and translator have been asserted

First published as *Lotta på Bråkmakargatan* by Rabén & Sjögrn Bokförlag
First published in Great Britain by Macmillan Publishing Company 1963
First Published in this edition 2008 by Oxford University Press

Database right Oxford University Press (maker)

British Library Cataloguing in Publication Data

Data available

ISBN 978-0-19-272757-2

1 3 5 7 9 10 8 6 4 2

Printed in Great Britain by Cox and Wyman Ltd, Reading, Berkshire

Paper used in the production of this book is a natural,
recyclable product made from wood grown in sustainable forests.
The manufacturing process conforms to the environmental
regulations of the country of origin.

Contents

Everyone is so horrid to Lotta

One day soon after her fifth birthday, Lotta woke up in the morning feeling cross from the very start. She'd had a dream that upset her, and she thought that what people dreamt must be real, silly little Lotta. And that was why she was cross.

'They hit my Teddy!' she screamed when Mummy came in to see why she was sitting in bed howling at eight o'clock in the morning.

'Who did?' Mummy asked.

'Joe and Mary-Lou,' screamed Lotta.

'Poor Lotta, you've just been dreaming,' said Mummy. 'Joe and Mary-Lou have gone to school. They haven't had time to do anything to Teddy.'

'They did it anyway, even though they didn't have time,' Lotta screamed, cuddling her poor Teddy.

Lotta's Teddy was a fat little pig her Mummy had made out of pink cloth and given her for her third birthday. Teddy had been clean and pink and beautiful then, but now he was dirty and in fact looked more like a real piglet. But Lotta thought he was a bear and that was why he was called Teddy, even though Joe said, 'Huh, that's not a bear, it's a pig.'

'Don't be so stupid,' said Lotta, 'of course it's a bear!'

'If you say so,' said Joe. 'But I'd like to know whether you think it's a polar bear or an ordinary brown bear.'

'I think it's a piggybear,' said Lotta, 'so you've got to as well!'

Lotta loved her piggybear. He slept in her bed at night and she talked to him a lot when Joe and Mary-Lou couldn't hear her. But now Teddy was lying on the pillow feeling sorry for himself because Joe and Mary-Lou had hit  him, Lotta thought. She cried and stroked Teddy and said, 'Poor Teddy, I'm going to give Joe and Mary-Lou such a slap, I am really!'

Joe and Mary-Lou and Lotta and Mummy and Daddy lived in a yellow-painted house on Trouble-maker Street, as Daddy called it. Every morning Joe and Mary-Lou went to school and Daddy went to the office. It was only Mummy and Lotta who stayed at home in the house.

'How lucky I am to have my little Lotta,' Mummy used to say. 'Otherwise I'd be on my own all day long.'

'Yes, you are lucky to have me,' Lotta used to reply. 'I'd feel very sorry for you if you didn't.'

But she didn't say that now, not this morning when she was so cross. She didn't say anything, she just sat there pouting and looking angry. When it was time to get dressed, Mummy brought her the white jumper that Grandma had knitted for her.

'Not that,' said Lotta. 'It tickles and scratches.'

'Of course it doesn't,' said Mummy. 'Feel how soft and smooth it is.'

'No, it tickles and scratches,' said Lotta without even feeling it. 'I want my vivid dress.'

She had a pale blue velvet dress which was kept for best. Lotta called it her 'vivid dress'. And she wanted it now, though it was only Thursday, just an ordinary Thursday.

'You can wear your velvet dress on Sunday,' said Mummy. 'Today you're wearing this jumper.'

'I'd rather not wear anything,' said Lotta.

'All right, do that, then,' said Mummy, and went back down to the kitchen.

Lotta stayed where she was, sitting in the bedroom, angry and undressed; well, not completely naked, of course. She had a little vest and a pair of pants on and her socks and shoes.

'No other clothes at all,' said Lotta to Teddy—he was the only person she had to talk to.

'Lotta, are you coming down to drink your chocolate?' Mummy called from the bottom of the stairs.

'Not likely,' Lotta muttered under her breath, still sitting there.

'Answer me, Lotta,' Mummy shouted. 'Do you want your hot chocolate or not?'

Lotta felt quite pleased. Mummy could go on wondering whether Lotta wanted her chocolate. Lotta had no intention of answering, and it gave her a lovely feeling inside not to answer when Mummy called.

But she was hungry and really wanted her chocolate, so when she had waited long enough, she picked up Teddy and went down the stairs, going very slowly, stopping on every stair. She didn't want Mummy to be sure whether she was coming to drink her chocolate or not.

'I'll see how I feel,' said Lotta to Teddy.

And so she made her way to the kitchen.

'Well, here you are at last,' said Mummy.

Lotta stood in the doorway pouting, so that

Mummy would know she still hadn't stopped being cross.

Mummy and Lotta usually had breakfast together in the kitchen. It was always so nice there. It was now too. The sun was shining in through the window and on the table was Lotta's own blue cup full of hot chocolate with a cheese sandwich beside it. Lotta usually talked all the time during the day, but now she didn't say anything. Mummy sat there reading the paper and didn't say anything either.

In the end Lotta said, 'I might as well drink some chocolate then, if I must.'

'No, you don't have to at all,' said Mummy. 'And anyway, you must get dressed first.'

Lotta was already angry of course, but now she was absolutely furious. How stupid Mummy was. She had nothing to wear, only a horrible jumper that tickled and scratched, and now nothing to eat either. Oh, how stupid Mummy was!

'You're so stupid!' Lotta screamed, stamping her foot.

'Now then, Lotta,' said Mummy, 'that's enough. Go up to your room and stay there till you're good.'

Lotta gave a howl that could be heard right over

at Mrs Berg's house next door. She went out of the kitchen door and up the stairs and into the children's bedroom screaming all the way, and Mrs Berg next door shook her head and said, 'Poor little Lotta must have a very bad tummy ache!'

But Lotta didn't have a tummy ache at all, she was just in a rage. And at the height of her rage she caught sight of the white jumper. It was lying on a chair looking even more scratchy than ever. Lotta let out another howl and threw the jumper to the floor. But then she fell silent. Because there on the floor right beside the jumper was a pair of scissors that Lotta used for cutting out paper dolls. Lotta picked up the scissors and silently cut a big hole in the jumper.

'It serves you right,' she said. 'Because you tickle and scratch.'

She put her hand through the hole. Oh dear, it certainly was big, and how awful it looked to

see a whole hand sticking out where there shouldn't be one. Lotta suddenly felt rather frightened.

'I'll say it was a dog that bit a hole in it,' she said to Teddy. She held up the jumper in front of her and gazed at it for a long time. Then she took the scissors and cut off one arm. 'I'll say he chewed it to shreds,' she said. She held it up again and took

another long look at it.
Then she picked up the
scissors and cut off the
other arm too.

'I've never seen a dog
like it,' she said.

But then she started to feel really scared.

She bundled the jumper up into a ball and stuffed
it in the wastepaper basket. She didn't want to see
it any more. At that very same moment her mother
called up from downstairs, 'Lotta, are you being
good yet?'

Lotta cried quietly to herself and said, 'No, not
at all.'

She clasped Teddy in her arms and held him
tight.

'Though it serves them right,' said Lotta, 'if
everyone's so horrid to me.'

That wasn't true, and Lotta knew it, but if

you cut a jumper to pieces, you need something or someone to blame.

'Yes, *everyone* is horrid to me,' Lotta said to Teddy. 'That's the only reason I cut things to pieces.'

She looked over at the wastepaper basket where the jumper was.

'But anyway, it *was* a dog,' she said.

Lotta leaves home

Mummy wanted to go shopping soon, so she came up to the children's room and said, 'Hurry up and be good now, Lotta, and put your jumper on, then you can come with me to the shops.'

Going shopping was what Lotta liked doing best. But the jumper she had to put on if she was to go lay in the wastepaper basket in shreds, so it was no wonder Lotta let out a new howl that could be heard right over in Mrs Berg's house next door.

'What on earth is the matter with you, Lotta?'

Mummy asked. 'If you're going to be such trouble all day, I'd better go to the shop on my own.'

And so off Mummy went. Lotta stayed sitting on the floor screaming and screaming till she could scream no more. Then she fell silent and started to think.

What was going to happen, Lotta realized, was that she would have to spend the rest of her life in the children's bedroom just because of that jumper. Everyone else would be going to the shops and to school and to the office and having fun, but Lotta would be left sitting on the floor of the children's room with no clothes on and all alone with Teddy.

'So we might as well leave home,' she said to Teddy.

Yes, it was perfectly possible to move—May,

Mrs Larsson's home-help, had moved. Because she didn't like it at the Larssons', Mummy said.

'And I don't like it at the Nymans',' said Lotta to Teddy.

The Nymans—that was Mummy and Daddy and Joe and Mary-Lou . . . and Lotta herself, of course.

'They're so horrid here at the Nymans',' said Lotta, 'that it will serve them right if we move.'

So Lotta decided to leave home straight away.

'We'll have to hurry before Mummy comes back,' she said to Teddy, 'or we won't be able to.'

But she didn't want to leave home without it being properly noticed. She wanted Mummy to know and to cry about Lotta moving out. So she picked up pen and paper and wrote a note to Mummy. Joe had taught her to read and write capital letters. It was quite hard, but she managed it, and this is what it said on the note:

I HAV MUVED OUT LUK IN THE WASTPAPABARSKIT

Which meant: 'I have moved out—look in the wastepaper basket.'

'Then Mummy will know why I've left,' said Lotta.

So she picked up Teddy and went out. Exactly as she was, dressed just in a little vest and a pair of pants and her shoes and socks. She went to the kitchen first and drank up her chocolate. She took the cheese sandwich and ate it in the porch.

Where will Lotta go?

It's all very well moving house, as long as you know where you're moving to. But Lotta had no idea.

'I'll ask Mrs Berg if I can live with her,' she said.

And so she threw Teddy over the fence between the Nymans' garden and Mrs Berg's and climbed over herself. Scottie, Mrs Berg's dog, barked when he saw them, but Lotta ignored him. She went in to see Mrs Berg.

'Hello,' said Lotta, 'could I come and live here?'

'Hello, Lotta,' replied Mrs Berg. 'I thought you lived at home with your Mummy and Daddy!'

'Yes, but I'm going to move out,' said Lotta. 'I don't like it at the Nymans'.'

'Well, well, then I can understand you'd want to move,' said Mrs Berg. 'But shouldn't you put more clothes on?'

'They don't give me any clothes or any food at the Nymans',' said Lotta.

Now it so happened that Mrs Berg knitted jumpers and hats and gloves to sell to people who couldn't knit themselves. And she popped straight across to her chest of drawers and pulled out a white jumper and put it over Lotta's head. It was slightly too big and fitted her almost like a little dress.

'How does that feel?' Mrs Berg asked.

'Nice,' replied Lotta. 'It doesn't scratch or tickle.'

'Good,' said Mrs Berg.

'Yes, it's really good,' said Lotta.

Then she started looking round.

'Where could I have my bed?' she asked.

'That's not so good,' said Mrs Berg. 'You see, Lotta, I don't really think you can live here with me. There's no room for any more beds.'

'Oh, dear,' said Lotta, 'I've got to live somewhere!'

Mrs Berg thought for a moment or two, and then she said, 'I think you should live all by yourself, Lotta.'

'But I haven't got a house,' said Lotta.

'You can rent my junk-loft,' said Mrs Berg.

There was an old shed at the bottom of Mrs Berg's garden, where she kept her lawn-mower and her rake and her spade and some sacks of potatoes and firewood and odds and ends. It had a loft in its roof where she stored old furniture and other bits and pieces.

'Just old junk,' she said. That was why she called it her junk-loft.

Joe and Mary-Lou and Lotta sometimes used to try and sneak up to her junk-loft simply to look at all the things in there. But Mrs Berg always caught sight of them and would call from her window, 'No, you don't! You can't go up there!'

Yet now here was Mrs Berg suggesting that Lotta

could actually rent her junk-loft, so it was no wonder Lotta was pleased.

'That's the best thing I've heard for ages,' she said. 'Can I move in straight away?'

'We'd better go and have a look and see what state it's in,' said Mrs Berg.

So she and Lotta went up to the junk-loft together. Mrs Berg shook her head at all the stuff.

'I don't think you'd want to live in all this mess, would you, Lotta?'

'Of course I would,' said Lotta. 'It's lovely here. And feel how nice and warm it is.'

'Rather *too* nice and warm,' said Mrs Berg, opening the little window to let in some fresh air.

Lotta ran straight over to it and peered out.

'Look, you can see the Nymans' house from here,' she said.

'Yes, it's a pretty house they've got, the Nymans, and a pretty garden.'

Lotta stuck her tongue out at the yellow-painted house where the Nymans lived.

'But I'll never have to live there again, ha ha, because I'm going to live here all my life.'

There was a small red-striped curtain up at the window.

'See, I've already got curtains,' said Lotta happily, patting the curtain. 'All I need is furniture.'

'Do you want to do everything yourself, or shall I help you?' Mrs Berg asked.

'You can help a little bit,' said Lotta, 'but I'll decide.'

'Go on and decide, then,' said Mrs Berg. 'What furniture would you like?'

Lotta gave Mrs Berg a big smile. This was more fun than she'd expected, and she was silly not to have left home ages ago.

'I'd like this,' she said, pointing at a small white chest of drawers.

'All right, you can have it,' said Mrs Berg.

'And that red table,' said Lotta.

'That's fine,' said Mrs Berg.

'And some chairs,' said Lotta. 'Are there any chairs?'

'Yes, though they're a bit broken,' said Mrs Berg.

'Doesn't matter,' said Lotta. 'What else is there?'

'You'll need a bed, won't you?'

'Is there one?' asked Lotta.

'Yes, of course,' said Mrs Berg. 'There's a children's

bed behind the packing cases and a doll's bed here somewhere too. My daughter used to sleep in it when she was a little girl.'

'In the doll's bed?' said Lotta.

'No, in the children's bed, of course,' Mrs Berg replied.

'Then I can sleep in it now,' said Lotta. 'And  Teddy can sleep in the doll's bed, then he won't need to squash up in bed with me. Are there any bedclothes?'

'Yes, a mattress and some pillows and a blanket, I think,' said Mrs Berg. 'But no sheets.'

'I don't care about sheets,' said Lotta. 'Let's arrange the furniture!'

So Mrs Berg kindly pulled out the furniture and helped Lotta to set up a special little room for herself. They put the table and chairs by the window, and the chest of drawers against one wall, with the bed against the other wall and the doll's bed next to it.

'It's exactly like a real room,' said Lotta.

Mrs Berg found an old rag-rug as well, which she put on the floor, and that made it even more of a room. She put up a speckled round mirror above the chest of drawers, and over Lotta's bed she hung a picture of Little Red Riding Hood and the wolf. Lotta thought it was beautiful.

'You've got to have pictures,' she said, 'or it isn't a proper household.'

Lotta used to say that when she grew up she would have corns on her feet like Mrs Berg and a 'household' like Mummy's. And now here she was looking round her very own room and smiling to herself.

'I've got a household of my own now,' she said.

'Yes, and there's no hurry to get corns,' said Mrs Berg.

'No, I suppose not,' said Lotta.

Then she sneezed three times in a row.

'It's very dusty in here,' said Mrs Berg, 'that's why you're sneezing.'

'It doesn't matter,' said Lotta. 'I can dust. Is there a duster?'

'Have a look in the chest of drawers,' said Mrs Berg.

Lotta pulled out the top drawer.

'Oh, my goodness,' she said, 'there's a doll's coffee-set here.'

Mrs Berg looked in the drawer too.

'Oh yes, that old coffee-set, I'd forgotten all about it.'

'It was lucky I found it, then,' said Lotta.

She put the coffee-set out on the table. It was white with tiny blue flowers on. There were cups and saucers and a dish and a coffee pot and a sugar bowl and a cream-jug. Lotta jumped up and down in delight.

'If Mary-Lou saw this, she'd go crazy,' she said.

'I can hardly believe that,' said Mrs Berg. 'See whether there's a duster in one of the other drawers.'

Lotta pulled out the next drawer, but there was no duster there, either. But there was a big doll with blue eyes and black hair.

'Ooh,' said Lotta, 'ooh!'

'Ah, if it isn't Violet Emily,' said Mrs Berg.

'Is that her name?' said Lotta. 'She's beautiful. Well, Teddy can't sleep in the doll's bed then, because Violet Emily will  have to sleep there . . . I *can* have her, can't I?'

'Yes, if you take great care of her,' said Mrs Berg. 'And of course she should sleep in her own doll's bed. Teddy will just have to make room for her.'

Lotta nodded.

'Yes, but he'd probably rather sleep in my bed anyway.'

'Look in the bottom drawer as well,' said Mrs Berg. 'There must be lots of doll's clothes there. I remember I never stopped making clothes for that doll.'

Lotta pulled out the bottom drawer as fast as she could, and there lay piles and piles of dresses and jumpers and coats and hats and underclothes and nightdresses for Violet Emily.

'If Mary-Lou saw this, she'd go crazy,' said Lotta again. She lifted out all the clothes and sat down in the middle of the floor and started trying them on Violet Emily. Mrs Berg had just found a torn towel that Lotta could use as a duster. But Lotta said, 'I'll do the dusting later on. First of all I have to make up my mind which dress is to be her best one.'

It was hard for Lotta to decide, because there were so many different dresses, red ones and blue ones and white ones and yellow ones, some striped and checked ones and some with dots and flowers on.

'The embroidered dress is the best,' she said in the end. 'She can keep that for Sundays.'

'That's right,' said Mrs Berg. 'Don't let her wear it every day.'

Then Mrs Berg patted Lotta on the cheek and said, 'It looks as if it's all set up here, so I think I'll go home now.'

Lotta nodded.

'All right. If you see the Nymans, tell them I've decided to live in my own house and am never coming back home again.'

'All right, I will,' said Mrs Berg, going down the stairs.

But when she was only halfway down Lotta called after her. 'Mrs Berg, I'll need some food as well!'

'Yes, of course,' said Mrs Berg.

'Could I have some from you?' Lotta asked.

'Yes, but you'll have to come and get it yourself, because I can't keep trotting up and down stairs.'

At that very instant Lotta caught sight of a basket hanging from a hook in the ceiling, and she shouted, 'Mrs Berg, see what I've found! I've had an idea!'

What Lotta had thought of was that she could tie a long string to the basket and lower it down from the window, and Mrs Berg could put her food in it.

'Then all I need do is pull it up, and hey presto, there's my food,' said Lotta.

'You're a clever little soul,' said Mrs Berg.

So off she went home to get some food for Lotta. When she came back Lotta had already lowered the basket and was sitting waiting.

'Hey presto, here's your food,' Mrs Berg shouted up.

'Don't tell me what it is,' Lotta shouted back. 'I want to see for myself.'

She pulled up the basket, and there was orange squash with two straws, and a cold pancake wrapped in paper and a small jar of jam.

'Better than at the Nymans', said Lotta. 'Bye, Mrs Berg. And thank you for the meal.'

Mrs Berg went back home. Lotta put the pancake on the table and poured plenty of jam on it. Then she made it into a roll and held it in both hands and took big bites out of it. In between bites she drank the orange squash through both straws.

'It's really cosy,' said Lotta. 'And no washing-up to do. Yet people say it's so hard running a household.'

Lotta didn't think it was hard running a household—just fun. When she'd finished eating, she wiped her hands on the duster.

Then she dusted her furniture, the table and the chest of drawers and the chairs and the bed and the doll's bed and the mirror and the picture of Little Red Riding Hood and the wolf.

 She made up the doll's bed for Violet Emily and the children's bed for herself and Teddy. She was so happy that she went round singing a little song that she knew:

'When the day's no longer light,
I close my little house up tight.
I make it cosy, warm, and bright,
My cat and I, alone at night.'

'Though I haven't actually got a cat,' said Lotta.

Lotta has Visitors

Lotta played with Violet Emily and Teddy and the doll's coffee-set for a long, long time, and dusted her furniture five times. But in the end she sat down on a chair and started thinking. 'Oh, dear,' she said to Teddy, 'what do people find to do all day long when they're running a household?'

Just as she said it, she heard someone coming up the stairs—it was Joe and Mary-Lou.

'I've moved,' she said.

'We know,' said Joe. 'Mrs Berg told us.'

'And this is where I'm going to live for the rest of my life,' said Lotta.

'That's what you think,' said Joe.

But Mary-Lou went rushing over to the doll's coffee-set.

'Oh!' she said, picking up the cups and the dish and the coffee pot. 'Oh!'

Then she saw Violet Emily and all her clothes.

'Oh!' she exclaimed, raking through the dresses to see how many there were.

'Leave them alone,' said Lotta. 'This is my house and they're my things!'

'Oh, can't I play here too?' said Mary-Lou.

'All right, though only for a little while,' said Lotta. Then she added, 'Is Mummy crying?'

'No, of course she's not crying,' replied Joe.

'Oh, yes I am,' Lotta heard someone say from the

bottom of the stairs, and suddenly there stood Mummy. 'Of course I'm crying for my little Lotta.'

Lotta nodded and looked very pleased with herself.

'Well, there's nothing we can do about it. I've moved into a new house.'

'So I see,' said Mummy. 'And how nice it all looks!'

'Yes, much better than at home,' said Lotta.

'I've brought a little flower for you. That's what you do when people move house,' said Mummy, giving Lotta a red geranium in a jug.

'What a good idea,' said Lotta. 'I can have it in the window. Thank you!'

Lotta dusted her furniture once again, so that Mummy and Mary-Lou and Joe could see her, and they thought Lotta was really good at running her own household. But when she'd finished dusting, Mummy said, 'Won't you come back home with Joe and Mary-Lou for dinner?'

'No, I get my meals from Mrs Berg,' said Lotta, and showed them how cleverly their basket arrangement worked.

'So you're not so stupid after all,' said Joe. And he sat down on the floor and started reading some old magazines he'd found in a corner.

But Mummy said, 'Goodbye then, little Lotta. If you feel like coming home again, maybe around Christmas-time, you know we'll all be pleased to see you.'

'How long is it till Christmas?' Lotta asked.

'Seven months,' Mummy replied.

'Huh, I'll definitely be here more than seven months,' said Lotta.

'That's what you think,' said Joe.

So Mummy left. Lotta and Mary-Lou played with Violet Emily and Joe sat on the floor reading his magazines.

'Isn't it fun here, Mary-Lou?' said Lotta.

'Yes, it's the best playroom there is,' said Mary-Lou.

'It's not a playroom,' said Lotta. 'It's my house.'

Then they heard someone else coming up the stairs—it was Daddy.

'Oh dear, oh dear, oh dear, what a terrible thing,' said Daddy. 'There's a story going about that you've left home, Lotta, can it be true?'

Lotta nodded. 'Yes it's true, I have.'

'Well then, I know someone who'll be crying tonight, and that will be your poor old father. Just imagine me coming into the bedroom to say good-night to all my children and finding one bed empty, and Lotta not there.'

'There's nothing we can do about it,' said Lotta. Though she felt sorry for Daddy, she really did.

'No, I suppose there isn't,' said Daddy. 'But Joe and Mary-Lou are coming home now anyway. We've got mince and stewed apricots for dinner.'

And off went Daddy and Joe and Mary-Lou.

'Goodbye then, little Lotta,' said Daddy as he left.

'Goodbye then,' said Lotta.

'Bye,' said Joe and Mary-Lou.

'Bye,' said Lotta.

'All alone at night . . .'

So Lotta was alone again. Mrs Berg brought her dinner. Lotta hoisted up the basket and there was another bottle of orange squash with two straws and a cold pork chop.

'Just as good as at the Nymans',' Lotta said to Teddy.

After she'd finished eating, she dusted her furniture again. Then she stood at the window looking over at the Nymans' house. Joe and Mary-Lou were out in the garden playing croquet with Daddy. The apple trees were in blossom and they looked like big bunches of flowers, Lotta thought. It was all very pretty.

'It's fun playing croquet,' said Lotta to Teddy, 'though not as much fun as running your own household.'

Soon it began to get dark. Daddy and Joe and Mary-Lou went indoors in their yellow-painted house. Lotta sighed. Now she had nothing to look at any more.

She'd been standing at the window gazing out for a long time, and meanwhile something had been happening to Mrs Berg's junk-loft that Lotta hadn't expected. It had grown quite dark, as she saw when she turned round. The darkness lay in the far corners of the loft, lurking there very black. But it came creeping closer and closer to Lotta's room, until there was just one little light spot left in front of the window.

'We'd better go to bed, or soon we won't be able to see anything,' said Lotta to Teddy.

She hurried to put Violet Emily to bed in the doll's bed and Teddy in the children's bed. Then she crawled in herself next to Teddy and pulled the blanket right up over her head.

'It's not that I'm afraid of the dark,' she said, 'but I do think it's very sad.'

She sighed a few times and then sat up and peered out into the darkness.

'Ooh,' she said, snuggling down under the blanket again. She hugged Teddy tight.

'Joe and Mary-Lou must have gone to bed now too,' she said. 'And Mummy and Daddy will be coming up to say goodnight. But not to me . . .'

She sighed again. And that sigh was the only thing to be heard in the whole loft, otherwise everything was absolutely, completely silent. It shouldn't be so quiet, Lotta thought, and so she began to sing.

'When the day's no longer light,

I close my little house up tight,'

she sang—but then fell silent and sighed.

She tried once more:

'When the day's no longer light,

I close my little house up tight . . . '

Poor little Lotta couldn't sing any more, she just burst into tears.

But then up the stairs came Daddy, and he was singing:

'I make it cosy, warm, and bright,

My cat and I, alone at night.'

Lotta cried even more.

'Daddy!' she shrieked. 'If only I at least had a cat!'

Daddy picked Lotta up from the bed and held her

in his arms. 'You know, Lotta, Mummy is so unhappy at home. Don't you think you could come back home for Christmas after all?'

'I want to come home *now*!' shrieked Lotta.

So Daddy took both Lotta and Teddy in his arms and carried them back to Mummy in the yellow house.

'Lotta has come back home!' Daddy shouted as soon as they came into the porch.

Mummy was sitting in front of the fire in the living room. She held out her arms to Lotta and said, 'Is it true? Have you really come home, Lotta?'

Lotta flung herself into her mother's arms and cried so much that the tears streamed down her face.

'Yes, I want to live here with you all my life!' said Lotta.

'Well, that's wonderful!' said Mummy.

Lotta sat on her Mummy's lap for a long time, just crying and not speaking, until in the end she said,

'Mummy, I've got another white jumper now, that Mrs Berg gave me. That's all right, isn't it?'

Mummy didn't answer, but just sat looking at Lotta in silence. Lotta hung her head and mumbled, 'I cut the other one to pieces, and I *want* to say sorry, but I *can't*.'

'Well, if I say I'm sorry too,' said Mummy, 'if I say sorry, little Lotta, for all the times *I've* behaved stupidly to *you* . . .'

'Yes, then *I* can say sorry,' said Lotta.

She threw her arms round her mother's neck and hugged her as hard as she could and said, 'Sorry, sorry, sorry, sorry!'

Then Mummy carried Lotta up to the children's bedroom and tucked her up in her own lovely bed that had sheets on it and a pink blanket that Lotta used to pull the fluff out of as she went to sleep. Daddy came up too, and he and Mummy both kissed Lotta and said, 'Goodnight, dear little Lotta.'

Then out they went.

'They're so nice,' said Lotta.

Joe and Mary-Lou were nearly asleep, but Joe said, 'I *knew* you wouldn't stay there all night.'

To which Lotta replied, 'But I'll go there during the day to play, so there. And if you dare hit my Teddy again, you and Mary-Lou, I'll give you both a real slap, so there.'

'We couldn't care less about your old Teddy,' said Joe. And then he fell asleep.

But Lotta lay awake for a while longer, singing to herself:

> 'When the day's no longer light,
> I close my little house up tight.
> I make it cosy, warm, and bright,
> My cat and I, alone at night.'

'Though that's not about me, it's about a different Lotta,' said Lotta.

ASTRID LINDGREN

Astrid Lindgren was born in Vimmerby, Sweden in 1907. In the course of her life she wrote over 40 books for children, and has sold over 145 million copies worldwide. She once commented, 'I write to amuse the child within me, and can only hope that other children may have some fun that way too.'

Many of Astrid Lindgren's stories are based upon her memories of childhood and they are filled with lively and unconventional characters. Perhaps the best known is *Pippi Longstocking*, first published in Sweden in 1945. It was an immediate success, and was published in England in 1954.

Awards for Astrid Lindgren's writing include the prestigious Hans Christian Andersen Award and the International Book Award. In 1989 a theme park dedicated to her—Astrid Lindgren Värld— was opened in Vimmerby. She died in 2002 at the age of 94.

If Lotta's antics had you in stitches, then don't miss the very first 'Lotta' book,

LOTTA SAYS 'NO!'

Here is an extract for you to enjoy...

Lotta is such a baby

My brother is called Joe and my name is Mary-Lou, and our little sister is called Lotta. Lotta is only just four years old. Daddy says that before there were any children in the house everything was perfectly peaceful. But afterwards there was a constant hullabaloo. My brother was born before me. And Daddy says the house was full of banging and screaming almost straight away, from the moment Joe was big enough to hit his rattle against the side of his cot while Daddy was still trying to sleep on Sunday mornings. And from then on Joe just got noisier and noisier. So Daddy calls him Big Shriek. And he calls me Little Shriek. Though I don't make as much noise as Joe does at all. Sometimes I'm quiet for ages. Then we got another baby, and that was Lotta. Daddy calls her Little Shrill, but I don't know why. Mummy calls us Joe and Mary and Lotta, our real names. Sometimes she calls me Mary-Lou, and so do Joe and Lotta.

We live in a yellow-painted house on a little street called Candlemaker Street.

'Maybe there were candlemakers living in this street once upon a time, but nowadays there are only troublemakers,' Daddy says. 'I think we'll rename it Troublemaker Street.'

Lotta is upset that she isn't as big as Joe and me. We're both allowed to go as far as the market all on our own, but Lotta isn't. Joe and I go to the market on Saturdays and buy sweets from the old ladies there. But we bring sweets home for Lotta too, just as we're told.

One Saturday it was raining so terribly hard that

we nearly couldn't go at all. But we took Daddy's big umbrella and went anyway, and we bought some red sweets. We walked home eating sweets under the umbrella and that was fun. But Lotta wasn't even allowed to go out in the garden because it was raining so terribly hard.

'What's it raining for?' said Lotta.

'So the wheat and potatoes will grow and we'll have something to eat,' said Mummy.

'Why does it rain on the market, then?' asked Joe. 'Is it to make the sweets grow?'

Mummy just laughed.

When we had gone to bed that night, Joe said to me, 'Mary-Lou, when we go to Grandma and Grandad's, let's not plant carrots in the garden—let's plant sweets instead, that'll be much better.'

'Yes, though carrots are better for our teeth,' I said. 'But let's use my green watering can to water them—the sweets, I mean.'

I felt really happy when I remembered my little green watering can that I had out in the country at Grandma and Grandad's. It was kept on a shelf in the cellar.

We always go out to Grandma and Grandad's in the summer.

Can you guess what Lotta once did out in the country at Grandma and Grandad's? There's a big dung-heap behind the cowshed, and Mr Johansson takes dung from it and spreads it on the fields to make things grow.

'What's dung for?' asked Lotta. Daddy said that everything grew extra fast if you put dung on it.

'And it has to have rain too,' said Lotta, because she remembered what Mummy had said when it had rained so hard that Saturday.

'Exactly,' said Daddy.

That afternoon it started to rain.

'Has anyone seen Lotta?' Daddy asked.

But we hadn't seen her for a long time, so we went looking for her. First we searched everywhere in the house and in all the wardrobes, but there was no sign of Lotta. Daddy started to get worried, because he had promised Mummy he would look after Lotta. In the end we went to search outside, Joe and Daddy and I, in the cowshed and in the hayloft and everywhere. Then we went behind the cowshed, and—what a surprise—there was Lotta standing in the middle of the dung-heap in all that rain, absolutely sopping wet.

'My poor little Lotta, what are you standing out here for?' said Daddy.

Lotta burst into tears and said, 'So I'll grow and be as big as Joe and Mary-Lou.'

Oh, Lotta is such a baby!

We play all day long

Joe and I play and play and play all day long every day. We let Lotta play with us too when we play the sort of games she can join in. But sometimes we play pirates, and then Lotta just gets in the way. She falls down off the table that we have as our ship. But she screams and wants to join in anyway. When we were playing pirates the other day and Lotta would-n't leave us in peace, Joe said, 'Do you know what to *do* when you play pirates, Lotta?'

'Stand on the table and jump up and down and be a pirate,' said Lotta.

'Yes, but there's a much better way,' said Joe. 'You lie on the floor under the bed absolutely quiet and still . . . '

'What for?' said Lotta.

'Well, you lie there being a pirate, saying very quietly over and over again, "More food, more food, more food",' said Joe. 'That's what pirates do.'

Eventually Lotta came to believe that really was what pirates did, and she crawled under her bed and started saying, 'More food, more food, more food.'

And Joe and I climbed up on the playroom table and sailed away to sea, though it was just pretending, of course.

Lotta lay under her bed all the time saying, 'More food, more food, more food,' and we thought it was almost as much fun watching her as being pirates.

'How long do pirates lie under the bed saying "More food"?' Lotta asked at last.

'Till Christmas,' said Joe.

At that, Lotta crawled out from under the bed

and got up off the floor and said, 'I don't want to be a pirate. They're stupid.'

But sometimes it's good having Lotta with us when we play. Sometimes we play at being angels, Joe and I. We're guardian angels, so we have to have someone to guard, and so we guard Lotta. She has to lie in her bed and we stand beside it swinging our arms and pretending they're wings we're flapping as we fly backwards and forwards. But Lotta doesn't think it's much of a game, because all she has to do is lie still. And when it comes down to it, it's not much different for her from playing pirates, except that then she lies *under* the bed saying 'More food'—otherwise it's the same.

We play doctors and nurses too. Then Joe is a doctor and I'm a nurse and Lotta is a sick child in hospital.

'I don't want to lie in bed,' said Lotta the last time we wanted her to be a sick child. 'I want to be a doctor and put a spoon down Mary-Lou's throat.'

'You can't be a doctor,' said Joe, 'because you can't write persciptions.'

'What can't I write?' said Lotta.

'Persciptions, like the doctor writes, to make sick children better,' said Joe.

Joe can write in capital letters, even though he hasn't started school yet. And he can read too.

At last we got Lotta to lie down on the bed and be ill in hospital, though she really didn't want to.

'So, how are we today then?' said Joe, sounding exactly like the doctor who came to see us when we had measles.

'More food, more food, more food,' said Lotta. 'I'm pretending to be a pirate.'

'Oh, you're silly,' shouted Joe. 'Let's stop, you can't play with us if you're going to be silly.'

And so Lotta let herself be ill in hospital, and we bandaged up her arm, and Joe held a big cotton reel to her chest and could hear through the hole in the middle that she was extremely ill in her chest. And he put a spoon down her throat and could see that she was ill there too.

'I'll have to give her an injection,' he said. Because once when he was ill he was given an injection in the arm by the doctor to make him well again, and that was why he wanted to give Lotta an injection. He went and got a darning needle that we pretended was the kind of needle that doctors have.

But Lotta didn't want an injection. She kicked her legs and screamed, 'You *won't* give me an injection!'

'You idiot, we're only *pretending*,' said Joe. 'Can't you see, I'm not really going to prick you?'

'I don't want an injection anyway,' Lotta yelled.

So we couldn't play doctors and nurses properly any more.

'I'll write out a persciption, anyway,' said Joe. And he sat down at the table and wrote on a piece of paper with a blue crayon. He wrote in capital letters, but I couldn't read it.

Joe and I like playing doctors and nurses. But Lotta doesn't.

SIK GURL MUST BE LOOKED AFTER. SIK GURL HAS TO HAVE INJEXION.
DOCTOR JOE MALM